About this book

Many children have difficulty puzzling out letters because they are abstract symbols. Letterland's worldwide success is all about its enduring characters who give these symbols life and stop them from being abstract. In this book we meet Naughty Nick. His story is carefully designed to emphasise the sounds that the letter 'N' makes in words. This definitive, original story book is an instant collector's classic, making learning fun for a new generation of readers.

A TEMPLAR BOOK

This edition published in the UK in 2008 by Templar Publishing
an imprint of The Templar Company plc,
The Granary, North Street, Dorking, Surrey, RH4 1DN, UK
www.templarco.co.uk

First published by Thomas Nelson & Sons Ltd, 1993
Devised and produced by The Templar Company plc

Copyright © 1993 by The Templar Company plc

1 3 5 7 9 8 6 4 2

ISBN 978-1-84011-766-0

Printed in China

Letterland © was devised by and is the copyright of Lyn Wendon
LETTERLAND® is a registered trademark

Classic **LETTERLAND**
Storybooks

Naughty Nick and the Nettle Nibbler

Written by Stephanie Laslett

Illustrated by
Jane Launchbury

templar publishing

There was a large crowd around the Letterland noticeboard. Naughty Nick was nailing up a big notice. Everyone gathered near, craning their necks to see what it said.

"The Letterland Riding Races will be held next week," said Naughty Nick. "Anyone who wants to enter must write their name here – nice and clearly."

"I will enter on my ostrich," declared Oscar Orange.
"And I will ride on my goat," giggled Golden Girl. Fireman Fred and Eddy Elephant decided to enter together.
Soon the noticeboard was full of names.

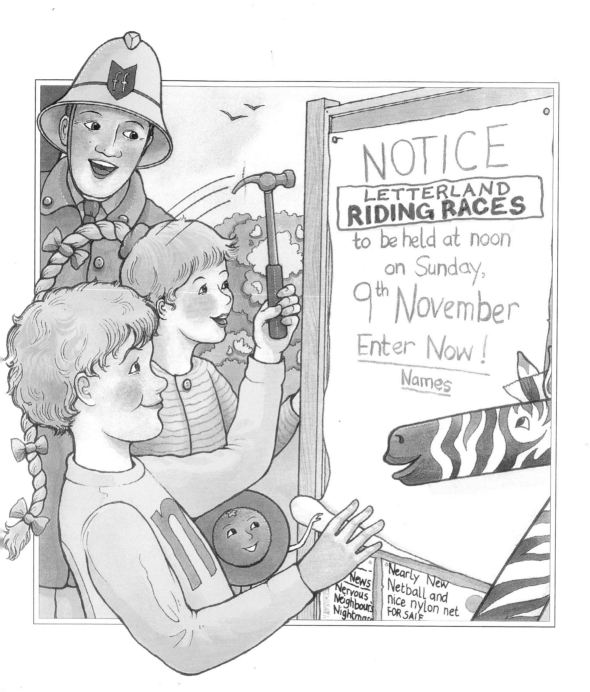

The Letterland Riding Races were always held in one of Fireman Fred's fields. The next day everyone set off to practise – the Hairy Hat Man on his horse, Henry, Oscar on his ostrich, and so on. In fact, nearly everyone from Letterland was there. Even the Quarrelsome Queen went along to watch.

But when they arrived, to their dismay they found that the field was knee-deep in nettles. Nettles as far as the eye could see.

"Oh no!" said the Hairy Hat Man. "There's no way that we can have the Letterland Riding Races here."

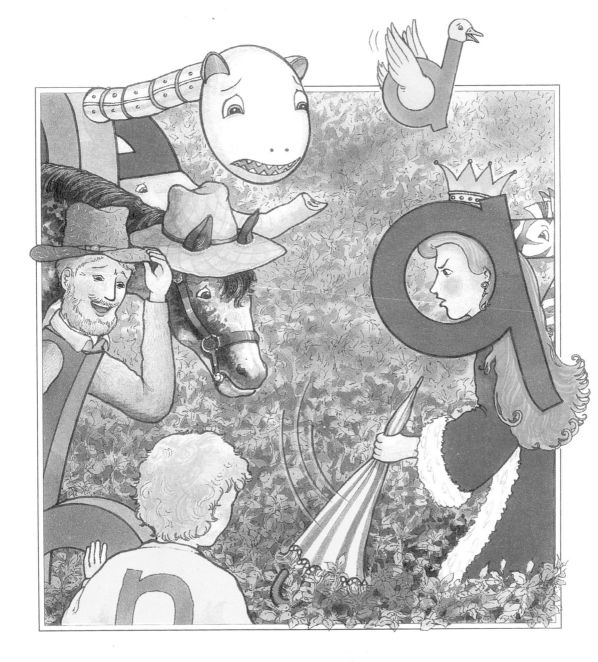

"**N**onsense!" snorted Quarrelsome Queen. "I'm not nervous of these nasty nettles! We can cut them down in no time!" But as soon as she tried, the leaves fell on top of her.

"Ow!" she shrieked, as a nettle landed on her nose. "This is horrible. No more nettles for me!"
"What a nuisance!" complained Fireman Fred. "How on earth can we get my field back to normal?"
"There's nothing we can do," sighed Poor Peter. "We'll never get rid of them in time."

Naughty Nick said nothing. He was too busy watching Doris the donkey.

She was nibbling the nettles just inside the gate. "Mmmm. Naughty… but nice!" she said, licking her lips. Everyone turned to look.

"Now, Doris…" said Clever Cat. "If you were to nibble non-stop, day and night, could you eat all the nettles in this field by Sunday?"

The donkey nudged the nearest nettle with her nose. She gazed across the field, then slowly swung her head from side to side.

"No. No, I'm afraid not," she sighed. "But it would be nice to try," and she began to nibble again.

"This is no good," sniffed Poor Peter. "We're getting nowhere."
"Never mind!" shouted Naughty Nick. "Now I know what we need!" And he ran off at high speed back towards his house.

For the rest of that day nobody saw Naughty Nick. But they knew exactly where he was. The noise from his workshop was deafening.
"What a racket!" complained his neighbours. "What *is* he doing?"

Night-time came but there was still no end to the noise. The next morning there was a notice on the workshop door.

"**N**O ENTRY!" it said. "To all my neighbours, near and far. Sorry about the noise, but I am working on a new invention. I know it is a nuisance… but it is necessary! PS. I need more nails!"

"What nonsense!" spluttered Sammy Snake. "This non-stop noise is giving me nightmares!" But there was still no sign of Naughty Nick.

Two days later the noise stopped. All was quiet and still. Kicking King called through the keyhole. "Naughty Nick! Are you in there?" But there was no answer.

Suddenly the doors flew open
and a *new* noise started up.
"Clanka, clanka, clink, clink,"
it went, and out through the doors
came the strangest sight,

"Now you can see my new invention,"
announced Naughty Nick proudly.
"Make way!"
He was sitting on top of an enormous
wooden machine. It had four big
wheels and, sticking out in front,
NINE gnashing sets of teeth.

"Strong teeth! Just like Doris the
donkey!" explained Naughty Nick.
"But my machine eats nettles nine
times as quickly!"

"It's marvelous!" exclaimed Munching Mike.
"It's super!" hissed Sammy Snake.
"It's FANTASTIC!" said Fireman Fred.
"It's nothing of the sort," replied Naughty Nick. "It's a Nettle Nibbler! Follow me!" and he set off down the road to the Race Field.

You could tell that the machine had been made by Naughty Nick because it was a little bit naughty itself! It took a bite out of the Hairy Hat Man's hat. It chewed up one of Jumping Jim's juggling balls. It even bit a hole in Robber Red's sack! "It's nearly as good at munching as me!" laughed Munching Mike.

Soon they reached the field.
Naughty Nick pulled a lever
on top of the Nettle Nibbler.
Everyone held their breath.
"Here goes," said Naughty Nick and he
pushed a large read button marked
'NIBBLE NOW'.

Suddenly the nine sets of teeth began
gnashing and nibbling through the
nettles as if the machine hadn't eaten
for months.
"Hooray!" cheered the crowd as the
machine chomped its way across the
field.

"Now we can have the Races after
all," giggled Golden Girl.

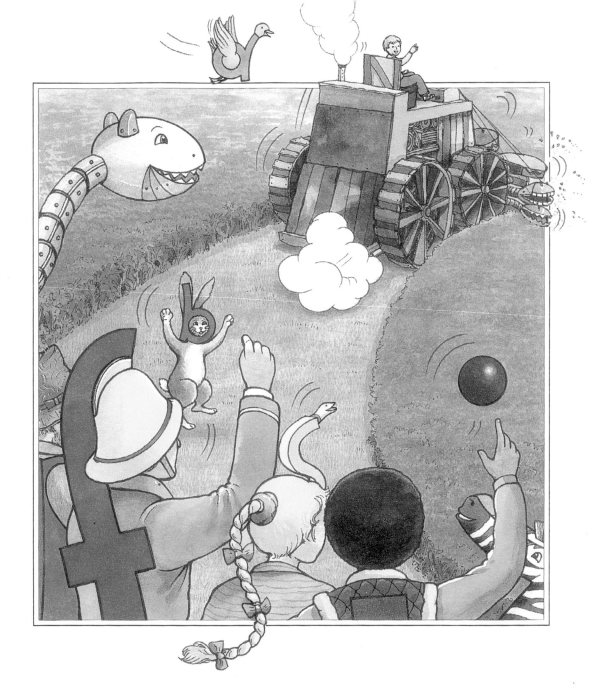

Sure enough, the Nettle Nibbler cleared the field in no time. It worked all morning and by the afternoon there was not a nettle to be seen.

"Well done, Naughty Nick," cried the Hairy Hat Man. "Let the Letterland Riding Races begin!"

Everyone lined up for the race to begin. Sammy Snake was the Race Starter.
"Ready, ssssteady, go!" he shouted and off they went, galloping down the field. Suddenly, from behind them all, came a strange noise.

"Clanka, clanka, clink, bonk!"
It was the Nettle Nibbler and
Naughty Nick! They streaked
down the field and crossed the Finish
Line just behind Oscar Orange.

Everyone cheered loudly and the
Hairy Hat Man cried, "Hooray, Oscar
Orange wins first prize!" But we now
need a special prize for Nick and his
Nettle Nibbler, too."

Can you guess what prizes they got?
A shiny new hammer for Naughty
Nick and a net full of nettles for the
Nettle Nibbler, of course.

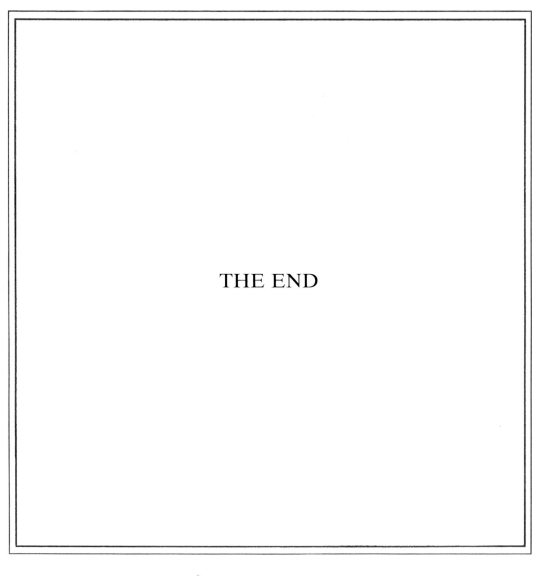

THE END